P9-DTY-104

CEDAR MILL COMM LIBRARY
12505 NW CORNELL RD
PORTLAND, OR 97229
(503) 644-0043

JUDY MOODY AND FRIENDS

WITHDRAWN
CEDAR MILL LIBRARY

Judy Moody, Tooth Fairy

Megan McDonald

illustrated by Erwin Madrid

based on the characters
created by Peter H. Reynolds

CANDLEWICK PRESS

In memory of Harry Weller

M. M.

To my niece, Vy Tran

E. M.

This is a work of fiction. Names, characters, places,
and incidents are either products
of the author's imagination or, if real, are used fictitiously.

Text copyright © 2017 by Megan McDonald
Illustrations copyright © 2017 by Peter H. Reynolds
Judy Moody font copyright © 2003 by Peter H. Reynolds

Judy Moody®. Judy Moody is a registered trademark of Candlewick Press, Inc.

All rights reserved. No part of this book may be reproduced, transmitted,
or stored in an information retrieval system in any form or by any means,
graphic, electronic, or mechanical, including photocopying, taping, and recording,
without prior written permission from the publisher.

First edition 2017

Library of Congress Catalog Card Number pending
ISBN 978-0-7636-9167-7 (hardcover)
ISBN 978-0-7636-9168-4 (paperback)

17 18 19 20 21 22 CCP 10 9 8 7 6 5 4 3 2 1

Printed in Shenzhen, Guangdong, China

This book was typeset in ITC Stone Informal.
The illustrations were created digitally.

Candlewick Press
99 Dover Street
Somerville, Massachusetts 02144

visit us at www.candlewick.com

CONTENTS

CHAPTER 1
Ooth-Tay Airy-Fay

Recess!

Judy Moody kicked the ball to Rocky. Rocky kicked the ball to Frank Pearl. Frank kicked the ball to Amy Namey. Jessica Finch ran into the circle and gave a wild kick.

Yipes stripes! The ball went flying through the air, hit a trash can, and rolled. . . .

Oh, no! Judy covered her eyes. She peeked through her fingers.

The ball rolled right over to a bunch of big kids. *Fifth*-graders.

Jessica looked at Judy.

"Don't look at me," said Judy. "I'm not getting it."

"I'm not getting it," said Rocky and Frank at the same time.

"Me neither," said Amy.

Gulp! Jessica Finch took one baby step, two jumping-jack steps, and three more baby steps. No giant steps.

"What's she doing?" Frank asked.

"She's stalling," said Amy.

"She's afraid of the big kids," said Judy.

"Me too," said Frank.

"Me three," said Rocky.

When Jessica came back, her face was so pale that her freckles stood out like chocolate chips in a cookie.

"Did you see a scary ghost or something?" Judy asked.

"Didn't see. Heard," said Jessica.

"You *heard* a ghost?" Rocky asked.

"Did the ghost say 'Boo'?" Frank asked.

Jessica shook her head and whispered, "No. But I have to tell you something. Something I heard. Something bad."

Everybody leaned in closer.

"There's no such thing as the ooth-Tay airy-Fay," she whispered in Pig Latin.

"What? There's no such thing as the Tooth Fairy?" Judy said.

"Who says?" asked Frank.

Jessica pointed across the playground. "A fifth-grader," she croaked.

"Maybe you heard wrong," said Amy.

"Maybe they didn't say *Tooth Fairy*," said Judy. "Maybe they said, *Bigfoot is hairy*. Or, *Mr. Todd is getting married*."

Jessica crossed her arms. "I know what I heard."

"But everybody knows there's a Tooth Fairy," said Amy Namey. "She's a teeny-tiny Tinker Bell who wears glasses, flies around on butterfly wings, and sprinkles fairy dust like glitter wherever she goes."

"And she has braces," Judy added. "Shiny, sparkly braces. The Tooth Fairy has to have perfect teeth."

"She carries a wand made of silver dental floss," said Amy. "And she's not afraid of the dentist."

"Her real name is Flossum Jetson," said Judy. "Flossie, for short. And when her wings get tired, she rides in a spaceship."

"No way," said Rocky. "Everybody knows the Tooth Fairy is a dude. He looks like a pirate and has an eye patch and flies with a cape."

"And he carries a surfboard,"
Frank added. "The Tooth Fairy is
a superhero, like the captain of
underwear. I know because I just lost
a tooth a few days ago." He opened
his mouth wide and showed them the
gaping hole.

"Did you put it under your pillow?"
Jessica asked.

Frank nodded. "I got two dollars,
two quarters, and sugarless
gumdrops."

"See? That fifth-grader was telling a big fat fib," Judy said. "He's a Fibber McGee. Everybody knows there's a Tooth Fairy. For real and absolute positive."

But her tummy did a little backflip. What if the big kid was right? What if the fifth-grader knew something she didn't know?

She, Judy Moody, was in a mood. A bummed-out, no-Tooth-Fairy mood.

Wait just a Flossum-Jetson second! She had an idea. It was as if she'd been sprinkled with fairy dust.

She, Judy Moody, would put the Tooth Fairy to the test.

All she needed was one loose tooth!

CHAPTER 2
Open Wide and Say "Stink"

Judy wiggled her front tooth. *Nothing.*
She wiggled her bottom tooth. *Zip.*
She wiggled all the baby teeth she
had left. *Zilch.* Not one wiggle. Her
teeth were stuck like glue.

Bingo! Judy knew somebody who
always had a loose tooth. And that
somebody just happened to be her
little brother, Stink.

"Open wide and say *ahh*, Stink,"
said Doctor Judy.

"Aaagghh!"

Judy shined her flashlight in Stink's
mouth. "You have a loose tooth all
right."

"It's been driving me crazy," said
Stink.

"Yep. It's time to get that bad boy
out of there."

Stink snapped his mouth shut. "No
way are we pulling my tooth out. Too
scary."

"But it's a *baby* tooth, Stink. Only *babies* have *baby* teeth."

"I'm not a baby," said Stink. "That's my shark tooth. See? My new tooth is growing in behind it, so I have *two* rows of teeth just like a shark." He made a shark face and clacked his teeth open and shut.

She, Judy Moody, had an idea. A throw-your-tooth-on-the-roof great idea.

"How about a snack, Stink?" Judy asked. They ran down to the kitchen. Apple. Dill pickle. Granola bar. Judy got out all the crunchy foods she could find.

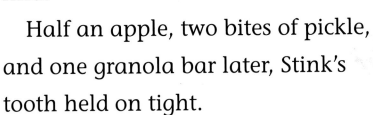

Half an apple, two bites of pickle, and one granola bar later, Stink's tooth held on tight.

"I know! Let's make snow cones!"
Judy got out her snow-cone maker
and added ice. *Presto!* In no time,
Stink was chomping on a nice icy
snow cone.

But even a nice icy snow cone did
not do the trick.

Maybe a sneeze would work? Judy sprinkled some pepper in her hand and blew it at Stink.

"*Ah-ah-ah-CHOO!*" Stink sneezed louder than a hippo.

But his tooth held on tight.

Maybe if Stink brushed his teeth? "Your breath smells like a vampire bat." Judy held out Stink's shark toothbrush.

Stink brushed his teeth. "How about now?" he asked, vampire-breathing on Judy.

"Still batty," said Judy.

Stink brushed his teeth a total of three times. But his tooth held on tight.

After that, Judy tried to make Stink laugh. Maybe if he laughed hard enough, his tooth would fall out.

"Stink, why did the vampire brush his teeth three times?"

"Because he had a loose tooth?"

"No, to prevent bat breath."

"Did you know that a hundred vampire bats can drink the blood of twenty-five cows in one year?"

"You were supposed to laugh, Stink."

"Oh. Hardee-har-har."

"What time should you go to the dentist?"

Stink touched his loose tooth. "I have to go to the dentist?"

"It's a joke, Stink."

"Oh. I don't know. What time?"

"Tooth-hurty."

"*Tooth-hurty?* Two thirty. I get it!" He let out a laugh, but his tooth held on tight.

She, Judy Moody, would just have to scare that loose tooth right out of him!

Judy hid behind the fridge. As soon as Stink walked by, she popped out and . . .

"BOO!"

"Aaagh!" yelled Stink.

"Let's see if I scared the loose tooth out of you," said Judy.

But scaring Stink just gave him the hiccups. "HIC!" Stink said, showing off his loose tooth.

Rats and double rats. That loose tooth sure was a hanger-on-er.

Judy had to think of a way to convince Stink to lose that tooth.

Cha-ching! All of a sudden, she knew just what to do. "Hey, Stink. You know how you want a lottery ticket?"

"If I can save five dollars, I can get Dad to buy me a scratch ticket with money bags on it. You scratch the money bags to find out how much moola you win."

"Think about it, Stink. If you lose your tooth, you can put it under your pillow and the Tooth Fairy will bring you lotsa money."

Stink's face lit up. "But the going rate for the Tooth Fairy is only three-seventy. That's not enough."

"You'll be three dollars and seventy cents richer than you are now. That's a lot closer to five dollars than *no* dollars."

"I'm in!" said Stink. "But I'm still not letting you pull my tooth."

"How about the old string-on-the-doorknob trick? You tie one end of the string around your tooth and the other end around the doorknob, then . . . SLAMMO!"

"No way!" said Stink.

Wait just a dill-pickle minute. Judy had an even better idea.

Before you could say *remote-controlled supersonic speedboat racer,* Judy filled the bathtub with water. She tied one end of a piece of dental floss to Stink's tooth, and the other end to his bathtub boat toy. "Ready, Freddy?" Judy asked.

"Ready as I'll ever be," said Stink.

"Motor boat, motor boat, go so fast. Motor boat, motor boat, step on the gas!" Judy turned the dial. The boat sailed around and around the bathtub. Judy revved up the engine. The boat zoomed faster and faster until . . .

YOINK!

Out popped Stink's tooth!

Stink's eyes bugged out. He stuck his tongue in the hole where his tooth had been. He grinned ear to ear.

Judy held up Stink's tooth. "What did the loose tooth say to the second-grader?"

"I don't know. What?"

"Nothing. They had a falling out!" Judy and Stink laughed their heads off.

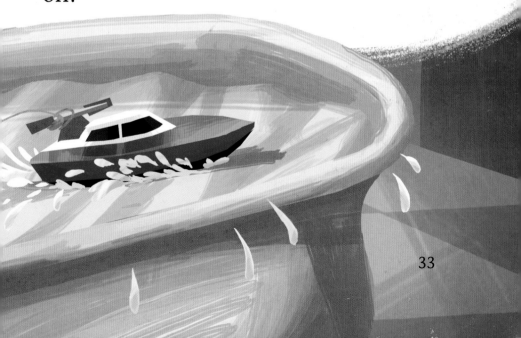

CHAPTER 3
Operation Tooth Fairy

Bedtime! Judy watched Stink put the tooth under his pillow. In no time, Stink was sawing logs. *ZZZZZZ!*

Judy waited up for the Tooth Fairy. Up periscope! She spied on the sleeping Stink. She read five chapters of her book by flashlight. She played cat's cradle all by herself: Eiffel Tower, Witch's Broom, Cat's Whiskers (for

Mouse). Oh, no! She fell asleep on top of her Cup and Saucer.

When she woke up, she checked *both* of her glow-in-the-dark watches. After midnight! She tiptoed over and felt under Stink's pillow. His tooth was still there.

NO TOOTH FAIRY!

What if the big-kid fifth-grade rumor was true? What if the Tooth Fairy was a no-show?

It was up to her now. Judy Moody,
Assistant Tooth Fairy, to the rescue!
She may not have sparkly braces or
fly with a superhero cape or wear
glasses, but she could be the Tooth
Fairy. All she had to do was put
money under Stink's pillow.

Judy dashed back to her room.
She checked her pockets. Empty. She
shook her piggy bank. Empty. She
dumped out her backpack. Empty.

Judy dug in her treasure box and pulled out her 1979 Susan B. Anthony one-dollar coin from Dad. It wasn't so shiny anymore. But it would have to do.

She slowly . . . carefully . . . slipped
it under Stink's pillow without waking
him up. Just then, Stink rolled over
and . . . Help! Her arm was stuck
under the pillow.

Judy couldn't reach the tooth without waking Stink. She had to give up.

The next morning, Stink woke up
and looked under his pillow. His tooth
was gone! And in its place was fake
money.

"Tooth Fairy! Tooth Fairy!" Stink
hopped out of bed and stepped on
something in his bare feet. "YOUCH!"
His tooth? Weird! What was his
tooth doing on the floor? Did the
Tooth Fairy drop it as she flew out the
window?

43

Stink ran downstairs to tell his family.

"Did the Tooth Fairy come last night?" Judy asked.

Mom's eyes got wide. Dad looked at Mom. Mom shook her head.

"Tooth Fairy?" asked Dad.

"We forgot to tell you," said Judy. "Stink's loose tooth, um, came out yesterday."

"Judy . . . bathtub . . . boat," Stink tried to say, but Judy held her hand over his mouth.

Stink pulled her hand away. "Something weird is going on." He held up his tooth. "The Tooth Fairy was here, but she dropped my tooth on her way out! All she left was this smelly old fake quarter."

"It's not smelly. And it's not a quarter. It's a real-not-fake 1979 Susan B. Anthony dollar," said Judy.

"Dollar?" said Stink. "Everybody knows the going rate for a tooth is *three* dollars and seventy cents."

"It is?" said Mom.

"It is?" said Dad.

"And," said Stink, squinting at the coin, "this looks just like the Susan B. Anthony dollar that Dad gave Judy—"

"Okay! Okay!" said Judy. "It was me, okay? I heard a big, fat, fifth-grade fib and I was afraid the real Tooth Fairy wouldn't come, so I put my Susan B. Anthony dollar under your pillow." Judy took a bow. "Assistant Tooth Fairy, at your service."

"You can't spy on the Tooth Fairy!" Stink wailed. "Nobody actually gets to *see* her. Mom! Dad! Judy scared the Tooth Fairy away."

"She'll be back," said Dad. "I bet she wants that tooth."

"Try again tonight," said Mom.

That night, Stink put the tooth under his pillow—again. "Operation Tooth Fairy, take two," he said.

Before he got into bed, he set a trap. A spy trap. A booby trap. A trick Dad had taught him. The old hair-on-the-doorknob trick to catch snoops and sisters.

He pulled a strand of hair
from a hairbrush. Then he set
the almost invisible hair on the
doorknob. If the hair fell off the
doorknob—*busted!*—Stink would
know for sure that Judy had come
into his room.

Stink tossed and turned and gave
his pillow a fluff, then a punch. Or
two. At last, he fell asleep.

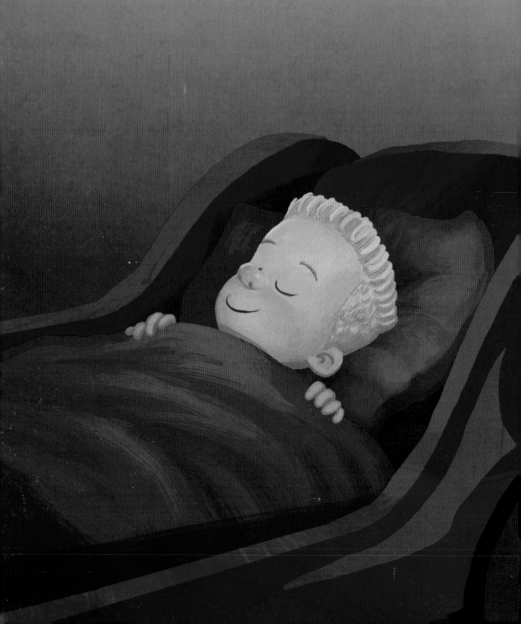

Judy crawled up onto her top bunk. She bit her nails. She finger-knitted up a storm.

She crossed and double-crossed her fingers. *Will the real Tooth Fairy pretty-please-with-sugarless-gumdrops-on-top show up tonight?*

As soon as Stink
woke up, he felt
under his pillow.
Cha-ching. Money!
Moola! Payola!

He hopped out of
bed and looked all
around for his tooth.
He looked on the
rug. He looked on
the floor. He looked
under his bed.

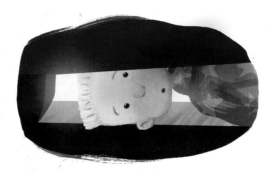

His tooth was G-O-N-E *gone!*

He raced over to the door. The hair was still there. The trick had worked! The Tooth Fairy was *not* Judy Moody, Assistant Tooth Fairy, this time.

"Tooth Fairy strikes again!" called Stink as he raced downstairs to tell his family. "Guess what. The real Tooth Fairy came last night. Guess what else." He waved some dollar bills in the air. "I got three whole dollars and seventy whole cents."

"Wow!" said Judy.

"Wow!" said Mom and Dad.

"Three dollars and seventy cents plus one Susan B. Anthony dollar from the Assistant Tooth Fairy makes . . . *four* dollars and seventy cents. All I need now is thirty more cents to make five dollars. Then Dad can buy me a lottery ticket."

"That dollar I gave you is from olden times," said Judy.

"It's from 1979," said Dad.

"Exactly," said Judy. "It's got to be worth at least thirty more cents."

"Yippee! Lottery ticket, here I come," yelled Stink. "Just think—I could win like a million dollars! Two million!" Stink pretended to toss money in the air. "I'm rich! I'm rich!"

"What did the rich kid say to his sister?" Judy asked.

"Bug off?" asked Stink.

"No. He said, 'I'll give you half my money.'"

"Hardee-har-har," said Stink.

Judy started to wiggle her teeth one by one.

"What are you doing?" Stink asked.

"Seeing if *I* have a loose tooth."

Judy Moody could not wait to tell her friends. The Tooth Fairy lives! For real and absolute positive.

Take that, fifth-graders!